SAVING CELESTE

INSTITUT FRANÇAIS
ROYAUME-UNI

This book is supported by the Institut français (Royaume-Uni) as part of the Burgess programme.

Also by Timothée de Fombelle:

Toby Alone

Toby and the Secrets of the Tree

Vango: Between Sky and Earth

Vango: A Prince Without a Kingdom

The Book of Pearl

Captain Rosalie

SAVING CELESTE

Timothée de Fombelle

Translated by Sarah Ardizzone

WALKER BOOKS

First published 2021 by Walker Books Ltd
87 Vauxhall Walk, London SE11 5HJ

2 4 6 8 10 9 7 5 3 1

This book has been typeset in Berling

Printed and bound in Great Britain by CPI Group (UK) Ltd

British Library Cataloguing in Publication Data:
a catalogue record for this book
is available from the British Library

ISBN 978-1-4063-9719-2

www.walker.co.uk

For Céleste

ONE

The first time she kissed me, we were dangling twenty metres above the ground, with fifteen armed men training their gun sights on us. Perhaps that's why, for a long while afterwards, looking at her made my head spin.

Today, I'm writing her name at the top of the only thing I have left: this small, damp notebook. I'm so cold that the fire hardly makes any difference. Why the ink hasn't frozen inside my pen is a mystery. There aren't enough pages to write this story as a book, but there's just enough space to record what happened, to leave a blue trace of something that changed my life, someone who might have changed the world.

Celeste.

I had made up my mind never to fall in love again. I came to this decision early on, aged six and a half to be precise. Picture a swimming instructor embarrassing a young child: "Don't stamp your feet! It makes you look like a dumpling being deep-fried!"

Most children would refuse to wear a swimming costume, or reveal an inch of flesh by the poolside ever again. Well, my response was to bury my heart under a heavy stone.

Before that, from the age of zero to six and a half, I used to fall in love with every passing pair of hair bobbles or buckle-up shoes, and it always turned out badly. I called it "toaster syndrome". I would feel my heart beginning to warm up nicely on both sides, until it suddenly flew into the air and landed – *splat* – on the floor.

But I *really* made up my mind to stop falling in love early one morning, as I was waiting for my croissant at the bakery on the seventy-seventh floor.

"Are you together?" asked the baker behind the counter, her gaze landing over my shoulder.

I turned around to see Charlotte, who was older than me. The colour drained from my face: I had a crush on this girl with her braces. I could already feel my toes scrunching in my shoes and my mouth turning as dry as the Kalahari Desert.

"Are you together?" the baker repeated.

She simply wanted to know if I was going to pay for my croissant and Charlotte's sweets at the same time. But her question had a whole other meaning for me, and it gave me goosebumps.

When I tried saying "no", the word got stuck in my throat. She might just have heard a tiny squeak like a guinea pig, if she was lucky. The toaster was heating up inside my chest. Charlotte smiled, revealing all the shiny metal bits of her braces.

"In your dreams..." she said with a smirk.

She slung the necklace of sweets around her neck and tossed a coin onto the counter.

That's when I made up my mind to stop, for good. Cross my heart, hope to die, I was never going to fall in love again.

The next day, I started drawing maps. I drew maps of the world across the walls of our apartment, and I played the piano. Nothing else.

For the next seven and a half years, that was all I did, apart from going to school, obviously, and having a few deep conversations with Bryce.

Bryce.

I'd like to have more space to write about Bryce. He deserves a long introduction, with memories crammed into the margins, but it's bitterly cold here, my notebook only has a few pages and I need to get on with the story...

Bryce lived in the Brick Towers District. His dad was a window cleaner who worked on the glass buildings in my district.

My address was !mmencity Tower, which was two blocks away from school. Every day at three-thirty, I'd leave school, take the three walkways down to Level 100, then cross and catch the lift up forty floors to reach home.

My apartment is big. Too big. I used to get

lost in it when I was little. You could have parked the Northern Express train in the hallway. There were seven guest rooms, but no guests.

Bryce would come over after school and we'd hang out together, while he waited for his dad who worked late into the night.

"Bryce!"

It was always the same scene, around midnight.

"Bryce!"

We'd catch sight of his dad in his green overalls, clipped to his window cleaner's gondola, calling out his son's name as he tapped on the glass. This was the signal for us to open up. We'd be greeted by sounds of the city snoring and a heady whiff of cleaning products. Bryce would climb into his dad's cabin.

"See you tomorrow..."

They glided down the glass wall, arriving back home deep in the night.

I liked Bryce's dad and his job as a soap-sodden acrobat taking flight among the skyscrapers. I liked Bryce, too.

Now I know that I owe them everything.

Bryce liked my mum, but he just said it to make me feel better. It's easier to like people you've haven't met.

You see, my mum was never, ever there. You could tell she was one of the bosses at !ndustry (a big cheese, as they say) by her hairstyle alone. She worked all hours, and she was always travelling.

I saw her once a month in the office waiting room.

Every Monday, she placed an online grocery order because she never wanted me to go without. The delivery man would ring the buzzer at ten o'clock at night and offload monstrous quantities of food: eight boxes, every Monday. I managed to get through three eggs, some pasta and a few broccoli florets each week, no more, before it started all over again. That fridge was a living nightmare. There was no way I could keep up.

Once a week, the telephone rang.

"Is everything all right, sweetie? Have you got what you need?"

This wasn't my mum, by the way. It was

her personal assistant, Gründa. My mum didn't have time to call.

Luckily, I had Bryce. He would work his way through the fridge while I drew my maps. After sixteen yogurts and a kilo of pistachio nuts, he thought he was almost on top of things, but then he'd remember all those marshmallows taunting him with their big pink eyes.

Every evening before he left, Bryce threw out a mountain of packaging. Even now, I can hear the sound of crushed plastic in the waste disposal system.

And I haven't forgotten my subscription to "Console Me!" Five games, paid for by my mum, appeared on the computer every Wednesday. Bryce helped me out by eating crisps and gaming for six or seven hours, while I practised the piano in my bedroom.

"Console Me!"? Even the name made me wince.

I've never taken piano lessons. I play what's in my head and in my fingers – melodies that haunt me. If I'd listened closely to what my fingers were playing, I might have suspected I didn't really belong to this world.

I never felt bored, though. Not once. Today, when I look back on it, the one thing my mum gifted me with – in leaving me to bring myself up – was a talent for never feeling bored.

Sometimes, I would remove the piano lid to see how the strings and hammers worked, then fall asleep at the keyboard, resting my head on its toothy grin.

Oh dear, I've filled several pages now without writing about what matters. Time to go faster. It's so cold and outside the wind is getting up.

So, as I was telling you, I had made up my mind never to fall in love again. But then *she* walked into my life on the day I turned fourteen. No one knew where she had come from before. Just that she and her parents were now living at the top of Tower 330. Tower 330 is the car-park tower in the Glass District, where the cars are stacked vertically, like books on shelves.

Looking back on it now, it seems crazy. Three hundred levels chock-a-block with cars arranged vertically. But at the time, I thought it was perfectly normal. It even seemed like a smart solution.

Perhaps that's what disturbs me the most. The fact that back then I thought the world I lived in was perfectly normal.

Celeste.

As I said, she appeared in the lift on the morning of my fourteenth birthday. We rode the rest of the way in silence.

Amazing Coincidence Number One: nobody else called the lift. It was like we were cut off from time. She smelled of earth warmed by the sun and I felt as if we might carry on rising for ever between the clouds, until we brushed against the dark side of the moon.

Amazing Coincidence Number Two: she stopped at the hundred and fifteenth floor, just like me, and walked into school, just like me.

I lost sight of her in the corridors.

Shortly before break-time, the principal entered our classroom.

"This is Celeste. Make her feel welcome!"

She was standing just behind him.

Bryce was absent that day. The previous evening, round at my place, he had eaten two whole boxes of popcorn. His seat was free because he was off sick.

She came to sit next to me.

Once, as a very small boy, I had visited the circus with my father, on the lower ground floor of !ntencity Shopping Centre. The lion tamer had made a black panther jump up on a chair that was close to me. All these years later, I sensed a similar tension in the air when Celeste sat down at the small desk next to mine.

"This is Celeste. Make her feel welcome!" the principal had said. But what I'd heard was: "Make her feel well. Come!" I had no idea why he was speaking in riddles.

At break, I scoured the school roof terrace for Celeste. I didn't realize she had stayed behind in class, to fill out a form. Leaning over the glass parapet, I kept saying to myself:

Don't fall, don't fall, don't fall.

I was so scared of falling in love.

At lunchtime, she left.

She never set foot inside our school again.

TWO

I let a few weeks slip by.

I remembered when I used to sprout lentils on cotton wool. The first few days were always the worst, because nothing happened. You just stared at the lentils. Even the cotton wool seemed to dry in slow motion, and you had to wait for ever before you could water it again.

Don't overwater the lentils, or they'll drown!

There are times in life when everything seems to take for ever.

During those early days without Celeste, I felt a keen sense of impatience. I had managed to live for fourteen years without her in my life. But now that I had spent less than half a morning in her company, one minute without her was worse than waiting for lentils to sprout.

The following day, Bryce was back at school. He thought I was behaving oddly and started writing me notes:

You're acting weird…

He was right. I felt weird.

I had flown out of the toaster, as had

happened so many times before, except that this time, I wanted to avoid a crash landing. This time, I decided to stay up in the air.

Just picture a piece of toast which, before touching the floor, starts flapping its wings, rising up again, hovering, brushing against the waxed tablecloth as it makes for the window.

Just picture a piece of toast *rebelling*.

That afternoon, I was drawing my maps.

I had been tackling Latin America for a couple of months now. I was painting all the information I had gathered from a dozen atlases onto a single map on my bedroom wall. The previous year, next to the bathroom door, I had finished Asia and three quarters of the Pacific, letting the Indian Ocean overflow onto the parquet floor.

Latin America.

I tried to keep focused, since it would only take a second's lapse in concentration for the top of Chile to run into Peru, or for me to miss a city with a million inhabitants living at altitude.

But my head was spinning with thoughts of Celeste. Sometimes I just stopped stock-still for a quarter of an hour, as I relived the moment when she had appeared in the lift. My paintbrush hung in suspended animation above Tierra del Fuego, as if someone had cast a spell on me or I had been paralysed.

"Can you hear me?"

"Huh?"

It was Bryce.

"I said, I've finished the freezer."

"I don't care about the freezer, you fat oaf!"

His face glowing, Bryce stood proudly before me, a dusting of sugar on his nose. Finishing the freezer on Friday evening meant he had beaten his record, scored a personal best. For the first time in our relationship, instead of thanking my friend, I had insulted him.

I watched his expression cloud over, before he turned his back on me and slammed the door.

I laid down my paintbrush and pressed my head against the wall, the red of Cuba no doubt seeping into my hair. I ran out of my bedroom and down the hallway, calling out

Bryce's name. I wanted to apologize.

"Bryce!"

When I reached the living room, I saw the window cleaner's gondola in front of the window. It was too late: Bryce had already joined his dad.

"Listen, Bryce!"

The gondola began its descent and they vanished.

The next day, I set off in search of Celeste.

Tower 330 is at the other end of the Glass District, another ten towers away. Outdoor travel is reserved for cars using the high-speed roads and tunnels, as well as the flyovers that loop in and out of each other like spaghetti.

So, my route was via the covered passageways and shopping centres.

It was a Saturday and the crowds would have been crazy, but I can hardly remember anything about my journey. I know I just kept walking through the throng towards Tower 330, head down, my eyes glazing over to filter out the flashing adverts on the shopping centre floors. I was trying to remember Celeste's face. I didn't know her surname. I hadn't even heard the sound of her voice.

I caught a glass lift, which also contained a grocery store, a bar and a shoe shop; this meant it descended slowly so that people could carry on shopping at their leisure.

!ntencity Shopping Centre is the largest shopping centre in the city. When you're inside one of the glass lifts, you can see across to where Tower 330 rises up out of its own cloud of smoke. I stared at the top of the car-park tower, wondering if Celeste was up there, somewhere in that grey smog.

The lift glided down to the basement, twenty floors below zero. Plenty of people stepped out with me. They were off to collect their cars. I followed the flow of pedestrians, all of them clutching bunches of plastic bags. Inside those bags would be other bags, containing even smaller bags, then more bags still. People love bags. All I had was two trouser pockets, with my fists inside.

"Car number?" asked the parking attendant.

"I don't have a number. I'm looking for my mum – I lost her somewhere up there. She'll be coming this way to collect her car."

"You don't have a mobile to call her on?"

He was staring at me as if I was prehistoric.

"No."

This time I wasn't lying. I've never owned a phone (and if I was a dog, I wouldn't want a lead either).

"Sit down over there."

I did as instructed. The bench, which was high and uncomfortable, was positioned close to a metal door. I waited and watched.

The parking attendant typed in each customer's number to activate the "eject" procedure: the car would then drop down from one of the three hundred floors, like cans in a vending machine. Drivers collected their cars from a little further off, via a shopping gallery where they would complete their collection of plastic bags.

Twenty minutes went by. Twice, I noticed customers who had forgotten their numbers being taken to one side as the attendant escorted them over to a biometric scanning device.

For the few seconds it took the attendant to run the scan, he had his back turned to me. Five seconds would give me enough time to act.

So, when a third customer forgot their number, I slid off my bench and pushed the metal door. It wasn't locked, and I disappeared into a passageway where the doors of a tiny lift opened. I punched 330 into the keypad and the motor whirred into action.

As the lift climbed speedily and noisily, I wondered how many times Celeste had taken this vertical path.

I dug out of my pocket the piece of paper that had brought me here. Celeste had left her information form crumpled up in the back of her school locker, after filling in her name and address. It's always the same format: the name of your tower followed by which level you live on.

Celeste had written: 330/330.

It only took a few seconds to rise one level, but at least fifteen minutes to reach the top. Cars stacked one kilometre high? Just thinking about it now gives me goosebumps.

When the lift doors opened, I was assaulted by dense smoke. The heat from thousands of car engines, across hundreds of floors, rising up in a greyish column…

As I strode out onto the roof terrace, I held my sleeve over my mouth in an attempt to filter the exhaust fumes. I was expecting the outside air to be more breathable than the air inside the shopping centre; but a thick smog hung above the tower, concentrating the pollution. The vast turbines installed on the roof didn't seem to have much effect.

"What do you want?"

A giant man in the obligatory worker's uniform of a cap and green boiler suit stood opposite me in the fumes.

"I'm looking for Celeste."

"What do you want?" he repeated, in his strange accent.

"I want to see her."

"Why?"

The question felt as odd as if someone had asked me why I wanted to live. What could I say?

"Celeste was at school with me."

The man drew nearer. He was tall, with a tool kit fastened to his belt, plus two bottles of water and some bread tucked under his arm. He looked like he was on his way home, but who could possibly live in such a place?

"There's no one called Celeste here."

"I need to see her. Then I'll leave."

He was standing next to me now, fixing me with his stare. I can't have done a very good job of looking dangerous, or big, or threatening in any way, because the closer he got, the less concerned he became. I coughed into my sleeve.

"There's no one called Celeste here," he repeated.

His tone was definitive. In normal times, I'd have given up. I had no right to be there in the first place. And clearly, I was no match for him: he was two heads and one cap taller than me. In normal times, I'd have turned on my heels and made my way back to the lift, my life, my piano, my maps.

In normal times.

But nothing felt normal any more. A tiny seed of madness began to germinate on that dark terrace. A wild plant sprouting and unfurling as it grew and stretched out its tendrils inside me. I realized that I was falling in love with Celeste.

I didn't even pause to draw breath before launching into the craziest sentence I could come up with on the spot.

"Tell her she's a thief."

I had plucked those words out of the air. They were nonsense and yet I knew they would lead me to the moment I'd been both dreading and craving. An enormous hand grabbed me by the collar and raised me up so I was level with the man's face.

"What did you say?"

"Celeste is a thief."

His eyelids twitched and his grip on my neck tightened.

"What did you say, boy?"

"I said, Celeste is a thief, but who cares since she doesn't live here?"

I don't have enough space in this notebook to explain how unusual it was for me to act the hero. Let's just say, I've never been the sort to pick a fight with men who are bigger than me, or smaller than me for that matter. I've never dared strike anything apart from the eighty-eight notes on my piano. Even as a small child, I had already given up on the idea of transforming the world. I painted it exactly as it was, on the walls of my bedroom, without making any changes…

Let's just say that flinging these words in the face of a giant, up on the three hundred and thirtieth floor, which I knew my mother would expressly forbid me from visiting, was a novel feeling.

"Celeste doesn't steal."

I smiled. The man spoke between gritted teeth and looked ready to strangle me, but what he had just said filled me with joy. Celeste did exist. And he knew her.

"I need to see her."

My captor must have detected the emotion in my voice because he put me down. As I loosened my collar and tried to breathe, he gave me a long, hard stare before heading off.

I was so focused on following the green boiler suit between the turbines that I could no longer smell the black dust hanging in the air. The man walked over to the edge of the roof terrace and opened a trapdoor.

Weak light spilled out. He muttered a few words in an unfamiliar language. I clambered in after him, down the rungs of a ladder set in concrete.

Eyes shone in the gloom. There was a woman.

"I'm looking for Celeste," I repeated.

The woman led me to a second tiny room, with even less light.

There, lying on the floor, shivering, her face pocked by a series of small marks, her arms and legs covered in bandages, Celeste was watching me.

THREE

"I recognize you."

No words came.

"I recognize you," she said again. "You're the boy from school."

Her pale lips traced a smile.

"What are you doing here?"

"I might ask you the same thing!"

"I think I'm sick."

She still looked beautiful.

"I think so too, Celeste. I think you're sick."

My eyes were smarting in the gloom.

"Why have you come here?"

"Because I missed you."

She could have smirked and said something like, "In your dreams..." or, "We've only met each other once..." or, "I don't even know your name..."

Instead, her response was: "I'm glad."

The woman, who I took to be her mother, had gone into the other room, from where we could hear the sound of subdued voices. I felt a painful twinge of happiness as I glanced at Celeste, lying on a mattress on the cold concrete floor. There was minimal furniture and a bare lightbulb hanging above her. From time to time, the giant's voice rumbled.

"That's my dad," she explained. "He's afraid we'll be thrown out of here if anyone finds out I'm sick. He's responsible for the upkeep of the ventilators on the terrace. It's a good job, with a living wage. He'd only just enrolled me at school, the day before this sickness set in. He was so proud..."

I stared at a mark on her forehead, a dark patch that looked vaguely familiar.

"Who's taking care of you?"

She gestured in the direction of her parents.

I couldn't take my eyes off that mark.

"Are you in pain?"

Her silence said it all. Every now and then, her body tensed in the shadow.

"Be careful," she said, when I leaned over her forehead. "It might be infectious."

We stayed like that for a while, not saying anything.

"I wasn't sure if you'd recognize me," I finally ventured.

"Well, I think you might be easier to recognize than I am, right now..."

She laughed a little while I tried to come up with a plan.

"Celeste. You mustn't stay here. I might have an idea. I'll be back tomorrow. Can I come back tomorrow? Can I? Please, Celeste?"

"I don't have the strength to say no," she whispered.

My fingertips brushed against hers and then I made my way back home.

* * *

"You know I'd love to put your mum on the line, sweetie, but she's in a meeting."

It was Gründa. From the bored tone in her voice and a faint scratching noise, I suspected she was filing her nails.

For the first time in my life, I was trying to get hold of my mother.

"Your poor mum's up to her eyes in work, sweetie. She's had the board of directors breathing down her neck since yesterday morning – you can't imagine the stress. We're trying to sign off the accounts for the end of the financial year. I'm afraid your call is bad timing."

She was right: given that I called my mum once every fourteen years, it was bad timing.

"Can you ask her to ring me back?"

"I'll tell her, sweetie, but don't count on her for much before the end of next week, or the start of the week after. She's not returning anyone's calls, not even the director general's. Just let me know if you need anything … the fridge will be filled tomorrow, Monday."

"I need to speak to my mum."

"Watch a good movie and eat a pizza."

Now, I would describe myself as calm, gentle and peace-loving, but I had a sudden urge to slide inside the telephone and force-feed my mum's personal assistant pizza through her ears.

"That's fine, Gründa," I said, adopting the most matter-of-fact voice on the planet. "It was just a minor health concern." And I hung up.

I knew that the word "health" would have a magical effect. Although I was never sick, my mum crammed enough medical supplies into our bathroom cabinet to open three pharmacies. For her, the only means of expressing her love was to worry about my health, and to dispense pills and capsules like she was firing them from a submachine gun.

"A minor health concern". I could rely on Gründa to pass on that kind of message. I sat down and counted to twenty.

Hey presto, the phone rang.

"Mum?"

"Thank goodness you're alive, sweetie. The !ntencity doctor is on his way. You gave me such a fright. Swallow the red pills with some water, and dissolve the blue ones. Lie down and—"

"Mum…"

"Take your temperature while you're waiting for the doctor. Place a hot-water bottle on your head and put some ice under your feet. There's a cough syrup that should help – you'll find it in—"

"Mum!"

"I don't have time, unfortunately. I've got—"

"Mum, listen. I'm not the one who's sick…"

Well, that stopped her talking, which was such a rare event I wasn't even sure she was still on the other end of the line. Then I did something I'd never done before. Actually, I did two things that I had vowed I'd never do:

I talked to her about my life and I asked her for help.

My mother works for !ndustry, which has the best private healthcare in the city. There are ten hospital floors at the top of !ndustry Tower, and all the leading doctors work there. When you own three thousand factories across the globe, as well as half the fuel oils market, you can afford a hospital or two to soothe your aches and pains. It's one thing to make other people cough, but you wouldn't want to catch a cold yourself, now, would you?

When I mentioned the roof terrace on top of Tower 330, I thought my mum was going to faint.

"I trust you didn't go up there?" she shrieked.

"I'll go there again tomorrow if you don't take care of Celeste."

"I forbid you from setting foot in that place, do you hear me? I absolutely forbid it!"

I held the phone away from my ear so that I was out of range of her spluttering.

"Do something, Mum," I said softly.

She began speaking to somebody on another phone. She must have forgotten to press the mute button because I could hear every word.

"Yes, Director General, I've still got my son on the other line. I'll be along shortly. You know what children are like ... I pride myself on the energy I put into my family.

It's ever so time-consuming, but what a joy … you see, the thing is, Director General, my son suffers from delicate health … I'll be with you presently."

She switched back to her conversation with me.

"OK. If it's the only way to stop you from doing something idiotic, I'll take care of this vagrant. When the doctor arrives, tell him to call me."

She hung up. I was over the moon.

It all happened so fast, just like in the movies. When Industry decides to do something, everything is in fast-forward mode.

The doctor rang at our door and

immediately called my mother, who was in a meeting. It was midnight. She issued instructions while he typed something on a small touchscreen and led me into the lobby area, where we took the lift. He had the code to access the roof of !ntencity Tower.

I could hear the helicopter approaching. We ran over the moment it landed, the wind blasting our hair. We were helped on board, where three more white coats were already seated inside, including two women doctors who smiled warmly at me. The pilot looked like a model in an advertisement for expensive watches. Within seconds, the air ambulance had taken off at a slight angle, leaving our stomachs on the ground.

The helicopter's searchlight swept the facades of buildings as we passed them. When Tower 330 appeared, we circled it twice and put on our face masks to help us breathe. Mine was too big, I discovered, after struggling to put on a high-vis vest. Everybody was speaking loudly and using thumbs-up signals.

"Lead the way," shouted the doctor, after we landed on the terrace.

"All right, Doc."

Just like on TV, the doctor, or "Doc", helped me to clamber out, while two medics followed with a stretcher. I ran towards Celeste's shelter and lifted the trapdoor, taking off my mask so that her parents would recognize me. They were trembling.

The doctors smiled at them and delivered more lines that sounded like they'd been lifted from a film script: "Everything's going to be fine", "It's all under control" and "Don't worry, we'll take good care of your daughter".

By this time, I was standing close to Celeste.

"What have you done?" she asked me.

"Don't panic, we've got this covered," I heard myself reassuring her, in the same kind of scripted dialogue as the others.

With no energy to resist, she let the team move her onto the stretcher. I realize now why emergency rescue operations on TV look like precisely choreographed dances: the victims are puppets the doctors must manipulate into the right position.

"We'll keep you updated," the team told Celeste's parents, on the way out.

The helicopter took off from inside the black cloud on the terrace. We could just glimpse the helpless couple down below, perched on their tower, between the turbines.

I held Celeste's hand. She still had that mark on her forehead. I racked my brains but couldn't think what it reminded me of. There were also more recent scars and something about their shape also felt familiar.

Celeste had fallen fast asleep.

When the pilot dropped me off at !mmencity Tower, the Doc thrust a swipe card for !ndustry Hospital into my hands, together with his business card, and bellowed that I was welcome to visit Celeste the following day and to call if I needed anything. It wasn't until the helicopter had taken off that I realized I hadn't returned my high-vis vest.

I waved at the air ambulance, but it was already flying off into the night, beaming its lights over the glass buildings. As my arms fell back by my sides, I didn't experience a sense of pride in what I'd achieved. Rather, I can still recall my body succumbing to an uneasy weariness that was less the result of exhaustion than a niggling sense of unease.

Sitting here now, with my notebook before me and this expanse of pure-white landscape all around, it strikes me that what I was experiencing was a premonition.

Deep down, as I watched the helicopter vanishing, I knew I had entrusted Celeste to a mechanical bird that might not carry her towards a soft and protective nest, but towards the most terrifying viper's lair.

FOUR

Hospitals rarely buzz with a party atmosphere, especially on Sundays.

You might see men in pyjamas wandering through reception in search of a coffee machine. Or families dressed in their Sunday best giving Great-Aunt So-and-So a peck on the cheek before heading home to real life and the lunch table, where they can pull up a chair and finally tuck into their roast chicken and potatoes smothered in gravy.

But this Industry Hospital was as entertaining as an amusement park. Even on a Sunday, it was full of people bustling down corridors, clowns performing in the cafeteria and waffle vendors touting their wares. Everything looked spotlessly clean. As I swiped my pass at the barrier, I realized my mum's offices were lower down in the same tower. It hadn't occurred to me to pay her a visit.

"Are you family?"

"Yes," I replied.

"What surname did you say it was?"

"I don't know her surname. But her first name is Celeste."

"Sorry?"

"She's called Celeste."

"You're a family member and you don't know her surname?"

"It's … it's a very … blended family…"

The receptionist gave me a funny look as she scrolled through the electronic records. I fiddled with the canvas bag slung over my shoulder; I had an atlas I wanted to give to Celeste.

"You're in luck. We've got a Celeste on the floor for global diseases."

I wasn't convinced this sounded very lucky. I'd have much preferred to hear there was a Celeste playing ping-pong in the garden.

"File 66-400," she added. "Room 221."

"Thank you."

I paced the corridors for several minutes before heading nervously to Room 221. After knocking twice, I opened the door to find an empty bed.

"She's in the examination room," said the nurse who had entered the room behind me.

"Can I wait for her?"

"If you've got the time."

"When will she be back?"

"Ask at the sister's desk."

At the end of the corridor, the sister was half asleep over her magazine.

"I'd like to know when the girl in Room 221 will be back."

"File number?"

"66-400."

"She's undergoing some tests."

"I know. When will she be back?"

"When she's finished."

The sister didn't bother looking up.

"Do you have any idea when that might—?"

"No. I don't have any idea about anything," she said noncomittally. "It's simpler that way. But you can take this envelope for the patient – it's from Dermatology. Give it to the doctor."

I slid the envelope into my bag, between the pages of my atlas.

"Goodbye," said the sister, who smelled of bleach and strawberry chewing gum.

I sat down in the corridor and soon began to drop off, worn out by the previous night. In one of my dreams I was at the controls of the helicopter, flying over the sea. Celeste was smiling next to me. She looked as if she'd made a full recovery. I was steering us low over the foam and spray to show her a whale when a flying fish leaped through the window and landed on her dress. She picked it up to return it to freedom and—

"Hey!"

Someone was shaking my shoulder.

"Are you still here?"

It was the sister again.

"Call these visiting hours?" she grumbled.

With no time to waste, I rushed back to Room 221. The door was ajar and I found a very old lady with wrinkles and a hairnet occupying Celeste's bed. This was clearly not Celeste, unless the situation was considerably more serious than I'd thought…

"We needed the room. Your friend won't be coming back," panted the sister, who had just arrived. "She's under priority observation, on the top floor."

"Can I go and see her?"

"No."

On my way out, I apologized to the patient in Celeste's bed.

"Don't waste your breath on Grandma here," said the sister. "She's as deaf as a doorpost."

It gets on my nerves when people talk like that.

"She must be a VIP, this girlfriend of yours, to qualify for priority observation on the top floor."

The sister spoke with a forced smile and a wink, as if I'd grown in importance in a matter of minutes. False flattery gets on my nerves, too.

* * *

I returned home feeling worried. What sort of state was Celeste in?

Sitting on the sofa, I took out the doctor's card. "Call if you need anything," he had said.

I rang the number.

"Yes?"

"It's me. How's Celeste doing?"

Silence.

"Can you hear me, Doc?"

"I can hear you. Don't concern yourself with the girl any more. It's better for you that way."

"Are you out of your mind?!"

"Forget Celeste. Consider this as some advice from a friend."

He hung up.

I called back.

"Where's Celeste? Tell me where she is!"

"Listen up," he said in a hushed tone. "I'm taking a risk just by answering your call, and I swear that's the truth. Forget about the girl."

Once again, it sounded unreal, like a line from a film.

The next time I called back, he didn't pick up. So, I phoned the hospital instead.

"Good morning, !ndustry Hospital, how may I help you?"

"I'd like to speak to the patient with file number 66-400."

"One moment please."

The operator spoke in a soothing voice, but I could hear the clatter of her keyboard as well as the irritating on-hold music. I'd have preferred to wait in silence.

"Hello?"

"Yes."

"I've just checked for you. There is no file number 66-400."

I gulped.

"So, she's left hospital?"

"No, sir, she was never here."

"I beg your pardon?"

"As I've just explained, that file number never existed."

I dropped the phone. The operator carried on in her soothing voice, but all I heard was hollow words.

I lay on the sofa for several minutes, reeling from the shock, before I made one final phone call.

"Gründa, put me through to my mother."

"Not now, my poor boy, the board of directors' meeting has just got underway. She'll call you back tomorrow. Are you feeling better, sweetie?"

"Gründa, put me through to Mum or I'll smash everything in her apartment."

"Well, let's see, sweetie..."

With a deft kick, I sent a porcelain vase flying towards my mother's display case of Bohemian glass ornaments. The sound effect was like hitting the super jackpot on a slot machine. I held up the telephone so that Gründa didn't miss the effect.

"Put me through to Mum."

One minute later, my mother was on the other end of the line.

"Mum, where's Celeste?"

"Calm down. You're overexcited. Who are you talking about?"

"Celeste! Where's Celeste?"

"I don't understand what you're saying. Who's Celeste?"

"The girl we took to hospital!"

"What girl, sweetie? Who are you talking about? I think you need to rest, my poor boy – you're worn out. Let's just forget all about this, shall we?"

This time, I sent the telephone flying straight through the plate-glass window. I figured I wouldn't be calling her again.

Two hours later, I was back at Tower 330 and climbing into the tiny, rattling lift, having pulled the exact same trick on the car-park attendant.

It seemed to take longer than ever to reach the top. I protected myself from the pollution by tying my jacket over my mouth and nose like a highwayman. As I climbed out onto the terrace, I ran towards the shelter where Celeste's family lived and opened the rusty trapdoor.

No lights. Nobody there to answer my calls. Nothing inside either: no mattress, none of the small pieces of furniture I had noticed the previous day, zilch. I slid down the wall into a crouching position.

What was going on? Celeste...? Had I dreamt everything? Was she just a figment of my imagination?

* * *

I set off again, this time with a pounding headache.

On Sunday evenings, the shopping centres finally close for a few hours. Fewer plastic bags patrol the city.

A man was playing the clarinet in front of a newspaper stand and I stopped to listen. It felt as if the music might break my heart. Perhaps my mum was right: I was tired; my knees were trembling. I would go home to bed. Forget all about this nightmare. When I thought about the mysterious disease, the helicopter, the doctors' smiles, rescuing Celeste … none of it seemed real. It was all too cruel and too extraordinary.

What about Celeste? How could I even

believe there might be someone like her in this world? I needed to sleep. My mind would be clearer after a good rest. I would pick up my life again where I'd left off. The morning before Celeste.

Just as I was about to walk away from the clarinet player, a photo on the newspaper stand caught my attention... My heart skipped a beat as I stared at the dark shape on the hoarding. It was like a large splotch of ink, or the outline of a heart that had been partially nibbled away. I closed my eyes, then opened them again: the dark stain was still there.

Celeste.

It was identical to the mark I'd seen on Celeste's forehead.

I blinked. The music had stopped. I went

over to the poster and read the caption below the ink splotch.

AMAZONIA. FAREWELL.

I took a deep breath. I had seen this image before: an aerial view of the last remaining hectare of Amazonian Rainforest. No bigger than a small wood or copse, cordoned off with barbed wire.

"If that was a person, we'd find a way to save them, wouldn't we?" said the musician behind me.

I spun around.

"What are you talking about?"

He paused a moment before pointing to the poster.

"The planet. If it was a person, we'd do everything we could to save it."

Sometimes, the simplest of sentences can change your life. I hugged the musician and broke into a run. I had never sprinted so fast. When I opened the door to our apartment, the lights sprang into action and I immediately spotted the canvas bag I had dropped there on my return in the small hours.

I picked it up and opened it, taking out the atlas I had meant to give Celeste. It was my favourite atlas, a small, cheap edition of a hundred pages or so, called *Atlas of a Fragile World*. I opened it and found what I was looking for: the envelope from the ward sister was still inside. I'd forgotten to hand it over.

I emptied its contents onto the table and an assortment of photographs spilled out: ten or so close-ups of Celeste's arms, neck, legs … there were marks almost everywhere, stains forming on her soft, smooth skin. In a magnificent full-face portrait, she smiled at the doctor who was taking her photograph. But it was the close-up of her forehead that confirmed my suspicions: the dark patch on it was exactly the same shape as that of decimated Amazonia.

Another photo caught my attention. On Celeste's shoulder, her skin showed signs of frostbite, clearly outlining…

I opened the atlas and turned the pages feverishly.

The Arctic Ocean!

My hand shook as I compared the photo and the atlas. What was visible on Celeste's shoulder was the melting Arctic ice...

In the minutes that followed, it all fell into place. The desertification of Africa, the submergent Indian coastline; all the ecological disasters around the world were displayed on Celeste's body. Every blow to our earth was being experienced by her. Her blood was as polluted as the seas and rivers, while her lungs were as contaminated as our cities. She was suffering from the same diseases as our planet, and she would slowly die of them.

I put my head in my hands. What had all those tests in the hospital been for? The Industry doctors must have reached the same conclusion as me and understood the ramifications: if anyone found out that a fourteen-year-old girl was experiencing, in real time, the damage we were inflicting on our planet – if news of this spread round the world – then nothing would ever be the same again.

And the first victim of this societal awakening would be the giant multinational that was polluting the entire world. The same multinational whose name was illuminated in flashing lights on top of the tower where Celeste was being held: *!NDUSTRY.*

For !ndustry to come clean about Celeste's disease would mean signing its own commercial death warrant. There was only one way out: make Celeste disappear.

"If that was a person," the musician had

said to me, "we'd find a way to save them, wouldn't we?" And this wasn't just any person, this was the girl I loved, so of course I would find a way.

Just then, I heard a tapping on the window of my apartment, and I glanced up to see a ghost.

"Bryce!"

FIVE

Monday night, midnight.

I was picturing the delivery man ringing my doorbell earlier that evening, only to discover there was nobody at home. No Bryce to benefit from those eight monstrous boxes. What a waste – something else to aggravate Celeste's condition.

For the past twenty-four hours, I had been viewing things differently and switching off lights whenever I left a room. I wanted to save her – my Planet Celeste.

Midnight, and my head was spinning with these kinds of thoughts as I navigated the control panel, inside a metal gondola, attached to a pulley system, scaling a gigantic glass building.

Industry Tower.

When Bryce had shown up at my place, on Sunday night, I could tell he'd forgiven me for my outburst.

Bryce didn't ask me for any kind of explanation. He could see the state I was in and wanted to know what he could do to help. I'm not altogether sure what Bryce is doing here on this earth. He's an angel. When I think about him now, I pray that life hasn't burnt his wings. I refuse to believe that kindness is a dangerous sport.

"Two things, Bryce. There are two things you can do for me."

Figuring that it might take us a while, he went to fetch a box of vanilla ice cream from the kitchen.

"Go for it…" he said, on his return.

"First of all, I need to send a message on the computer."

He smiled at me – a big, friendly, vanilla smile – knowing I didn't have the faintest idea how to operate that machine. I must be the only boy alive whose fingers have never touched any keyboard other than a piano.

Bryce sat down in front of the screen.

"Right. Who do you want to send it to?"

"Quite a lot of people."

"How many?"

"Nine billion."

Bryce was too polite to look astonished.

"It might take a while," was all he said.

"Can you do it straight away?"

"We'll have to make it go viral."

"Meaning?"

"I send a message that keeps reproducing itself until it goes ballistic."

"Ballistic?"

He paused and wiped the ice cream from his chin.

"You want to send this to everybody, right?"

I nodded.

"What's your message?"

I held out the photos.

"I'll do this from my place. Promise."

I trusted him implicitly. Did I dare to ask him the second favour? I needn't have worried because Bryce beat me to it.

"And the other thing?"

"Your dad cleans the windows of !ndustry Tower, right?"

"Yes."

"I could do with his help."

And that's how, on Monday night, I came to be in a window cleaner's gondola, scaling the tallest of tall buildings. Bryce's dad had met me at the foot of !ndustry Tower to show me how the controls worked.

"I hear you're not very switched on when it comes to technology?"

"I should be able to manage it."

We shook hands and Bryce's dad explained that he would be waiting for me in his van. Not daring to glance down at the void below, I made a rapid ascent and reached the top floor on the dot of midnight.

Before me was an empty room lit by a red lightbulb. I opened the window using the triangular key Bryce's dad had given me and felt my head spinning again, but for different reasons, as I set foot on the white tiled floor. This was the giddiness of fear: knowing that everything would play out in a matter of minutes.

I crept over to the door and peered through the porthole. Given the number of security guards in the corridor, I surmised that Celeste was still under priority observation. Another quick glance revealed a door at the far end of the corridor, guarded by four more men dressed in black who didn't exactly look like nurses. Celeste was in there, I was sure of it now, but how could I gain access to her room?

No time to think.

Somebody was fumbling with their keys on the other side of the door. It swung open just as I made it safely back inside the gondola, but I'd left the window ajar. Noticing the draught, the keyholder walked over to the window and closed it again without spotting me; he then turned his back and proceeded to handle the test tubes on a table. This way was blocked.

There was only one thing for it, I decided, as I reached for the controls: I was sure that Bryce's dad had said the gondola could also move sideways. Slowly, the gondola stirred into motion, sliding across the tower towards Celeste's room. What did I have to lose?

Sitting here now, chilled to the bone, I can still remember the powerful warmth that enveloped me when I saw her, my tears flowing, and a feeling of surprising strength.

Propped up by pillows on a metal bed in the middle of an empty room, Celeste hadn't seen me. There was no healthcare equipment, no sign of any treatments, nothing.

Those in charge knew that her recovery didn't depend on any kind of medical intervention, but on our actions: on every choice made by every country, by every company and by every single one of us on every continent. Her life was hanging in the balance, and it could be saved not by one single doctor, but by the collective *action* of human beings. Celeste was the only hospital patient in the world whose well-being could be guaranteed if *all of us* decided to make it happen.

She didn't look surprised to see me as I came closer. You'd have thought I was just back from taking the bins out or walking the dog, while she'd dozed off.

"Is it cold outside?" she asked, stretching.

"A little bit. We'll take your blankets with us."

Helping her to her feet, I was relieved to see she could walk. The only time I had to lift her was when it came to climbing through the window, and this proved easy, too easy. I couldn't help wishing she weren't so worryingly light.

The gondola began its descent and, for a moment, we felt like passengers in a hot-air balloon.

Celeste whispered a "thank you" in my ear as the night-time clouds reflected in the towers. I told her I didn't need her thanks, so she shifted the position of her lips and kissed me instead.

That was the moment the first shot was fired.

Two armed men stood at the window of Celeste's hospital room, while four others scrambled over the rooftop with automatic rifles. Shots ricocheted off the bulletproof glass, sending sparks flying into the night sky like a grand finale at a fireworks display.

From the bottom of the gondola, Celeste and I examined the four cables that prevented us from crashing to the ground: they were holding strong for now.

We'd already made it three quarters of the way down, but I was worried the !ndustry men would take the lifts and catch us at ground level.

A fresh explosion rang out. This time our gondola lurched dramatically, and all the window-cleaning equipment flew out of the cabin. I grabbed Celeste's shoulder to stop her joining the brushes, squeegees and bottles in the void. Something must have given way in the pulley system because our gondola was plummeting at a rate of several floors per second. We were now guaranteed to reach ground level before our pursuers, but in what state?

"Why did you tell my father I was a thief?"

I'll never understand how Celeste had the presence of mind to ask a question like that, while hurtling in free-fall down a skyscraper.

A thief, why had I called her a thief?

"I don't know. I made it up."

I remember I had wanted to provoke a reaction in her father, but there had also been some truth in the words I'd uttered so instinctively. When Celeste first appeared in my life, she had robbed me of my independence, my childhood, my carefree existence. She had left me with nothing but empty pockets, and the desire to be with her. Not that I held this against her, quite the opposite, in fact: thanks to her, I was now living life with my eyes wide open.

Living? As the ground rushed up to meet us, I had to admit we couldn't take staying alive for granted … I hugged Celeste more tightly.

"Are we landing?"

"Yes, Celeste, we're landing."

What followed wasn't the din or bump I'd been expecting. Nothing. Just a violent braking action that forced us to the bottom of the gondola.

Then silence. The peaceful silence I experienced in Celeste's arms, for the split second I had my eyes closed. Was this paradise? If so, eternity proved short-lived because a man grabbed hold of Celeste. I lashed out by kicking him in the face. In return for breaking his nose, I received a blow to the head and lost consciousness. Blackout.

* * *

When I came to, Celeste was sitting next to me in the cab of a van that was speeding along. The driver, who had stuck a piece of cloth over his nose with medical tape, was bleeding profusely.

Bryce's father.

"Did I break your nose?"

"Yes."

"I'm sorry, I thought—"

"Don't worry about it."

Briefly, Bryce's dad explained how the gondola's free-fall had been slowed by a security system installed at ground level, which he had managed to activate just in time. He didn't dwell on the way I'd thanked him, or the blow he'd dealt to my head so as to calm me down.

I glanced behind us to find there was nobody on our tail.

"I'm a fast driver," Bryce's dad explained.

So I'd noticed. The truth is, he was driving like a madman. The traffic lights were a blur, but we seemed to be heading in the right direction.

"Look!"

The first brick towers appeared. Despite all the dust and noise, I liked this district. The cityscape alternated between red and gold, according to the light and the colour of the bricks. The towers were linked by wooden planks thrown up to form criss-crossing walkways. Everything looked precarious and improvised, including the flow of pedestrians. Life was harsh in these brick towers, where workers made no distinction between day and night. Basements were often flooded by the river; nets were hung from the windows to protect against rats.

Celeste was sitting very still next to me, her eyes closed, until a left tug on the steering wheel made her slump against my shoulder. The van took a road which spiralled upwards inside a blackened tower. By the time Bryce's dad had switched off the engine, I was dizzy and Celeste was awake.

"Here we are," announced Bryce's dad, getting out of the van and walking round to open the door on Celeste's side. At almost twenty-four stone he was even heavier than his son. But I watched him lift Celeste by the waist, and out of the vehicle, with the grace and agility of a dancer.

She whispered her thanks and then I led her by the arm, the two of us walking beneath an enormous steel entrance. The van was already revving its engine behind us.

Central Station.

The station was on the fiftieth floor of the tower. It felt like a pressure cooker, heating up, steaming and whistling; except that, instead of kitchen aromas, what assailed your nostrils was the smell of hot metal against metal. Whichever way you looked, platforms and railway tracks were squeezed in tightly, while a grey crowd threaded its way through the maze.

"Don't worry," I reassured Celeste, who

didn't look worried. Nobody appeared to have noticed her white nightgown, which scarcely hid the wounds on her body. We were just a young couple limping through the main concourse, and nobody gave us a second glance.

A few minutes later, we had a compartment of the Northern Express to ourselves. I helped Celeste to lie down on the seat, then collapsed opposite her and heaved a sigh of relief: the hardest part was over. Through the steamy window, it was still possible to glimpse passengers wandering up and down the platform. The whistle would shortly blow and we would be off, headed for safety.

Thud. A face flattened itself violently against the glass and I leaped towards Celeste. Two giant hands framed the enormous features peering into our compartment.

The man recognized me through the steam and smiled: it was Bryce's dad again. He was shouting something, but I couldn't hear because the train was beginning to pull out of the station. I tried to force open the window as he ran along the platform, signalling with his hands:

"Bryce just called me. You asked him to send something on the computer..."

"Yes!"

"Photos, I think..."

Bryce's dad was sweating profusely as he weaved between the people on the platform.

The train was moving swiftly now and his voice began to rasp.

"He won't be able to send them. The … the cyber detectives tracked him down. They came to … to the house. They've taken away the computer and … and the photos…"

"What about Bryce?"

He stopped at the end of the platform. Our train gathered speed and this twenty-four-stone man in his green overalls was reduced to a tiny green pea, far away, at the edge of the railway track.

I turned back to find Celeste fast asleep on the seat.

In one sense, she was lucky … she didn't know, as I did, that our only hope had just vanished, along with the steam from the train and the whistling on the platform.

The name of our destination was printed in capital letters on the two tickets in my hand: NORTH TERMINUS.

SIX

I've written "6" at the top, but there are hardly any pages left. Although each part of this story deserves its own chapter, I won't make it to the end of this one … I had hoped to dedicate all of it to the girl who is resting beside me.

Here, in our wooden cabin propped between two trees, winter lasts all year long. The forest is all around us and I never grow weary of it: the snow and the frost, the white coat it wears, the murmur of snowflakes as they fall to the ground. I love the way the cold grabs my hand and numbs it. Life may be frozen and difficult in this place, but it means us no harm, and that's why I'm not afraid of the battle for survival.

Those first months in our remote hideout, I watched over Celeste the way I used to watch over the lentil sprouts of my childhood. I was terrified of her condition deteriorating, and I monitored the surface of her skin as if the enemy might rise up at any moment.

I knew that Bryce had failed in his mission: it hadn't been possible to send my message out into the world. So, I waited, expecting to see the destruction of the planet imprinting itself further on Celeste's body.

With one eye on the patient, I built our cabin and organized the rhythm of our life. Celeste helped me, too, as, little by little, she was able to walk outside in the snow more often. Her cheeks grew rosy. You'd almost have thought she was improving. I wanted to make time stand still, so we could enjoy this fragile miracle. How could I possibly have understood that time really was on our side?

One morning, as I scrutinized her face, I noticed that the mark on her forehead seemed to have shrunk ever so slightly. The following month, I was sure of it. It took me nearly a year before I could really believe what was happening.

Today, I find myself writing these words at

the bottom of my last page: *Celeste is slowly recovering.*

In this place, far from any other human beings, a single question bubbles up inside me: what about the world? How is the planet doing, if Celeste is getting better?

On one of those photos, now lost for ever, I had written in red felt-tip pen a message for humanity: *Celeste is my planet – let's save her.*

And what about tomorrow? Perhaps they'll track us down in the end. Perhaps they'll destroy us just as they've been wanting to for so long. Or perhaps a storm will wipe us out.

Anything could happen here. All I ask is this: if you find these pages, please make sure you give them to Celeste's parents.

End of the notebook

A wooden cabin built between two trees. A man approaches, armed with a double-barrelled rifle; he has left his snowmobile a hundred metres off.

Advancing cautiously between the trees, he observes a fine column of smoke wafting from the chimney. The place is inhabited, the snow around the house well-trodden.

The man, who has a frozen beard, takes a small box from his pocket and presses the red button, sending a satellite signal for reinforcements. He leans with his back against the cabin, straining his ears until he can just make out a regular creaking sound. He can't tell whether these are footsteps, or the flames in the fireplace. He crouches down to pass under the window without being seen, then glances furtively around. He spots somebody inside by the fire, a pencil in his hand and a notebook on his lap.

The man stands in front of the door and loads his rifle. In one movement he throws himself against the door, forcing it open with his shoulder. He enters, spins round, then aims his weapon at a girl lying under some blankets.

"Don't move!" he shouts.

He seems nervous.

"Where's he gone? I saw someone else."

The girl stares at him.

"You've found me," she answers. "Take me. I'm alone."

The man peers into the gloom, as if there's something he doesn't understand.

A shadow suddenly rises up behind him and rolls through his legs, grabbing hold of his rifle after causing him to stumble.

In a matter of seconds, the man is disarmed by a sixteen-year-old boy who points the rifle at him. The notebook lies on the floor.

"You're not having her," says the boy. "She's starting to get better."

The man stares at the girl. He bites his lip, unable to take his eyes off her face.

"You're the..."

Tears wet his frosted eyelids.

"You're … Celeste?"

She looks at him. She's never seen this man before in her life.

"I don't know you," she says.

"That's right," the man confirms. "Nobody knows who I am. I'm just a trapper from the North. Why would anyone know my name? But you…? The entire planet knows about you, Celeste."

The silence in the cabin has become electric.

The boy lowers his weapon to listen to the trapper.

"Everybody knows your story. You've changed the world…"

If the girl seems surprised, her companion has suddenly turned very pale.

"Bryce…" he whispers. "Bryce must have succeeded after all. The photos—"

"The photos are everywhere," the trapper interrupts. "Something extraordinary has happened. Everything has changed. People no longer go about their lives the way they did before. And … what about you, Celeste… Have you … recovered?"

As Celeste stands up, the blankets fall to the floor and she wraps her coat more tightly around her.

"Yes, I'm doing better. But what about our planet?"

A broad smile lights up the trapper's face. The smile of a doctor greeting parents when their child is finally out of danger. The smile of a notifying officer informing the next of kin that a soldier has survived, against the odds. The dazzling smile that accompanies the happy announcement of life's big news.

"What about our planet?" Celeste asks again, her eyes shiny.

The man smiles, takes a long, deep breath and begins to speak.

READ OTHER BOOKS BY TIMOTHÉE DE FOMBELLE...

TOBY ALONE

He's just one and a half millimetres tall, but Toby Lolness is the most wanted person in the great oak Tree. Pursued across a hazardous terrain of falling leaves, thick moss forests and bark mountains, hunted by an army of angry woodcutters and bloodthirsty soldier ants, Toby faces an epic battle for survival in an unforgettable miniature world.

"To take one tree as emblematic and bring it alive in great detail is imaginatively rich and great fun." *Guardian*

TOBY AND THE SECRETS OF THE TREE

The world of the great oak Tree is on the brink of devastation under the control of the power-crazed Leo Blue. Leo is inflicting fear and poverty throughout the Tree, capturing anyone who tries to resist and destroying the very bark on which they live. But Toby has returned – and he will find a way to fight back.

"You'll never look at a tree in the same way again… An unprecedented success." *Le Figaro*

Vango, Book One: Between Sky and Earth

Fleeing from the police and more sinister forces on his trail, Vango must race against time to prove his innocence – a journey that will take him to the farthest reaches of distant lands. Can Vango uncover the secrets of his past before everything is lost?

"Exciting, unusual and beautifully written."
David Almond

Vango, Book Two: A Prince Without a Kingdom

Vango has spent his life abandoning his loved ones to protect them from the demons of his past. But the mystery of his identity has started to unravel, and in the shadows of war and persecution, the truth will finally come to light.

"A distinctive and atmospherically cinematic tale."
Independent

CAPTAIN ROSALIE

In this astonishingly-drawn wartime story, a little girl called Rosalie is a captain on a very secret mission – a mission to learn how to read. Mother reads often to Rosalie, especially when Father sends them letters from the front line. But as Rosalie gets further along in her mission and begins to piece together the words in her father's letters, the truth about the consequences of war are finally and irrevocably revealed.

"A perfect little book about war, grief and peace that packs a mighty punch." *The Times*

THE BOOK OF PEARL

Joshua Pearl is from a world that our own no longer believes in. He knows that his great love is waiting for him in that distant place, but he is trapped in our time. As his memories begin to fade, he discovers strange objects; tiny fragments of a story from a long time ago. Can Joshua remember the past and believe in his own story before his love is lost for ever?

"A stunning example of the power of quality storytelling that will entrance young adult readers." *Young Post*

Sarah Ardizzone is one of the most sought-after translators working today. Her work ranges from picture books and graphic novels to fiction for all ages. She has won several awards including twice receiving the Marsh Award for Children's Literature in translation: for *Toby Alone* by Timothée de Fombelle and for *Eye of the Wolf* by Daniel Pennac. To find out more about translation as a creative process, Sarah recommends the WorldKidLit blog, the Stephen Spender Trust, Shadow Heroes and Pop Up Projects. Born in Brussels and based in Brixton, Sarah lives with her documentary filmmaker husband and young son.

Timothée de Fombelle is a celebrated author and playwright who achieved international success with his stunning debut, *Toby Alone*, and its sequel, *Toby and the Secrets of the Tree*. The series was translated into 28 languages and has won numerous awards, including France's prestigious Prix Sorcières and the Marsh Award for children's literature in translation. His gripping mystery-adventure series, *Vango, Between Sky and Earth* and *Vango, A Prince Without a Kingdom* gained international praise, and the first novel received an English Pen Award for translation. Timothée's other books include the beautifully imagined, *The Book of Pearl* and the compelling wartime story, *Captain Rosalie*, which was illustrated by Isabelle Arsenault. Known for his compelling and beautiful writing style, Timothée de Fombelle is a best-loved voice in Children's Literature and beyond.